This book is dedicated to my friend, Kathy Billings.

Thank you for sharing your editing skills, making creative suggestions, and encouraging me. This book is so much better because of you!

Brittah's Sparkle & Joy Club

Written by
Sharalyn Morrison-Andrews

Illustrated by
Lucas Richards

Brittah is a very happy dog
- full of sparkles and joy!

Brittah's brother, Lincoln, loves her merry spirit. He loves to play music and dance with her.

It makes them happy - full of sparkles and joy!

Each morning Brittah jumps out of bed, dances, and says:

"Today is a happy day
Sparkles and joy will come my way
And when they do
I will say thank you!"

Brittah told Lincoln that she wants everyone to feel full of sparkles and joy just like she does.

Lincoln said,

"Oh, that's easy! All you need to do is be kind to others.

It will make you feel happy too."

Brittah has many friends because she is so nice.

She would like you to meet them.

First, there is Ralph. He has the longest legs Brittah
has ever seen on a dog!

Brittah can walk right under him!
Ralph is very kind to everyone. He is a gentle giant.

Gus is the youngest in the group. When he
was a puppy he hurt his paw.

Now he can only walk on three legs, but this
hasn't slowed Gus down one bit.

He loves to run and play with all of his friends.

Hiker is Brittah's most talented friend. He knows lots of tricks!

His best one is dancing with his mom. When his mom plays their song, Hiker does a special routine with her.

Mimi is small, fluffy, and white.

Along with playing with her friends, Mimi loves to walk on
the beach with her mom and take afternoon naps.

Velvet has very soft fur just like the fabric.

She is very sweet and gentle which you can see
when you look into her big, brown eyes.

Finn is a very happy dog. He is always wagging his tail
and loves to go on walks with his family.

Finally, there is Rocco. He likes to sit on his porch in the sunshine and watch people walk by.

Brittah hopes her friends will help her spread sparkles and joy so she forms a club.

She calls it...

Brittah's Sparkle & Joy Club

The club meets in Brittah's doghouse. Each meeting begins with a dance and then they say the club motto:

During sharing time each dog tells what they did that week to spread sparkles and joy.

Mimi says that she saw a little girl in a stroller lose her teddy bear. Mimi ran, picked up the teddy bear and took it back to the family. The little girl smiled at her.

Ralph saw an elderly lady carrying her groceries while trying to cross a busy street.

He took the grocery bag and let the lady lean on him so they could cross the street together.

Once safely on the other side the lady patted Ralph's head.

Hiker went with his mom to the hospital to visit the children there. He did all of his tricks.

The children smiled and clapped their hands when Hiker had finished.

Finn played with his little brother, Sebastian, while their mom made dinner for the family.

Sebastian thanked Finn with a treat.

Rocco, Velvet, Gus and Brittah made paw prints with nice sayings and hung them on their neighbors' mailboxes.

The dogs agree that being kind and helpful makes them feel happy and thankful.

They know that they have spread sparkles and joy to others!

When the meetings are over they all enjoy some doggie treats.

Every day each of the dogs jump out of bed saying their club motto:

"Today is a happy day
Sparkles and joy will come my way
And when they do
I will say thank you!

And when they go to bed they remember the kind acts that brought sparkles and joy to others and made them feel thankful that day.

Would you like to become a member of **Brittah's Sparkle and Joy Club?**

The dogs would love to have you join them.

All you have to do is start each and every morning saying the club motto and then do something kind for someone during the day.

Each and every night as you drift off to sleep remember and give thanks for the helpful favor you did.

Join us in saying the club motto:

"Today is a happy day
Sparkles and joy will come my way
And when they do
I will say thank you!"

Brittah's Sparkle & Joy Club

Membership Certificate

For the many acts of kindness, being helpful to others, and for always being thankful. This certifies that

_____

is now an official member of

Brittah's Sparkle & Joy Club!!!!

Brittah
With Lincoln

Ralph

Gus

Hiker
With Sharalyn

Mimi   Velvet

Finn
With Sebastian

Rocco

Sharalyn grew up in Hallowell, Maine and was bitten by the "travel bug" at a very young age. While she loved to travel as a young woman, it was her marriage to David, whose job frequently takes them out of the country, that made travel a vital part of her life.

Over the years, Sharalyn has enjoyed writing by keeping a journal and, most recently, a blog. Her new interest is writing children's books about dogs she has known and the important life messages they impart to children.

When not traveling, Sharalyn and her husband make their home in Maine.

You can follow Sharalyn on her website at www.sharalynlovesanimals.com.

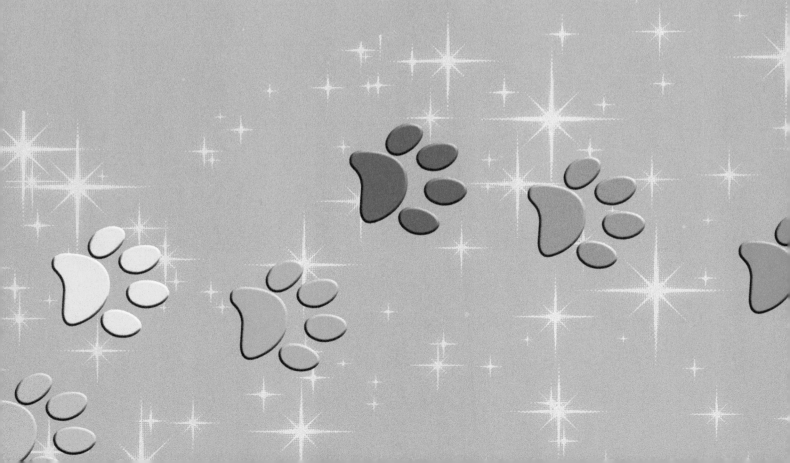

Lucas grew up in Cape Elizabeth, Maine. His aptitude as an artist emerged early in life. One could find him drawing on anything he could reach in his family's home.

His studies and passion for travel have allowed him to visit some of the world's best art museums, experiences that influence his style today.

9 780996 288958